SPINE SHIVERS

RAINTREE IS AN IMPRINT OF CAPSTONE GLOBAL LIBRARY LIMITED, A COMPANY INCORPORATED IN
ENGLAND AND WALES HAVING ITS REGISTERED OFFICE AT 7 PILGRIM STREET, LONDON, EC4V 6LB -
REGISTERED COMPANY NUMBER: 6695582

WWW.RAINTREE.CO.UK
MYORDERS@RAINTREE.CO.UK

TEXT © CAPSTONE GLOBAL LIBRARY LIMITED 2016

ISBN 978-1-4747-0818-0 (PAPERBACK)

19 18 17 16 15

10 9 8 7 6 5 4 3 2 1

BRITISH LIBRARY CATALOGUING IN PUBLICATION DATA
A FULL CATALOGUE RECORD FOR THIS BOOK IS AVAILABLE FROM THE BRITISH LIBRARY.

THE GRIN IN THE DARK

BY J. A. DARKE

TEXT BY ERIC STEVENS

ILLUSTRATED BY NELSON EVERGREEN

raintree

a Capstone company — publishers for children

CONTENTS

CHAPTER 1

Hamid Abdi leans his head on the passenger's-side window. He stares out at big houses and winding streets and the amber-glowing streetlights of his aunt and uncle's wealthy neighbourhood. The radio is turned to the local news station. The announcer is talking about the storm that's supposed to hit New Brighton tonight.

Hamid and his mum are on the way to his Uncle Mohammed and Aunt Julie's house. It'll be Hamid's first time babysitting for his twin seven-year-old niece and nephew, Afifa and Ahmed.

It's Saturday night. Hamid would much rather be hanging out with friends, playing video games. But he wants a game system of his own, and that means he needs money. And that means he has to babysit tonight.

"They *are* paying me, right?" he says towards the driver's seat, turning away from the window. It's not the first time he's asked his mum this question. "This isn't going to be considered a favour I'm doing, is it?"

"Hamid," his mum says. He can hear the smile in her voice.

"This isn't going to be good old Hamid helping out," he says, "like when I spent three hours weeding with Uncle Mo and then he made me pay for my own milkshake?"

Mrs Abdi laughs. "That's my brother," she says. "But don't worry about that. I talked to Julie, and you're definitely getting paid."

"Good," says Hamid.

"Julie says it's going to be a late night.

They're going to a benefit for the charity she works for. Dinner, drinks, music," Mrs Abdi says as the car climbs up Sycamore Hill Road.

The news announcer clears her throat. "I've just received an important alert," she says. "Especially for our listeners in Washington and Lincoln counties, north of the city of New Brighton."

Mrs Abdi wrinkles her forehead and turns up the radio. "What's this?" she says, concerned.

"Washington County authorities said moments ago that Josiah Pryce has escaped from the state prison in Fish Falls," the newsreader says. "Josiah Pryce is unstable and violent."

"Oh my," Mrs Abdi says.

"What?" Hamid asks, looking at his mum. "Should we be worried?" He knows Washington County is further north.

"Oh, of course not," Mrs Abdi says. She smiles and switches off the radio. "My guess is that the police will have him back in his cell within the hour."

Hamid watches the dull yellowish shine of the headlights slide across his aunt and uncle's house. It's huge and white, with giant windows that reflect the headlights and streetlights so they look like huge, wet eyes.

"Anyway, Julie said that she and Mo probably won't be back till midnight or later," Mrs Abdi says as she guides the car up the sloping, smooth driveway.

Hamid has always been jealous of that driveway. He can imagine starting at the top on his bike and gliding down the perfectly smooth drive towards the street. Then again, as his mum always reminds him, he would have to pedal back up eventually.

Still, compared to the bumpy, cracked

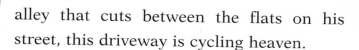

alley that cuts between the flats on his street, this driveway is cycling heaven.

Mrs Abdi parks the car and swivels in her seat. "Mo will drive you home tonight," she says. "There's no way I'm staying up past midnight. I have to work in the morning."

"Okay, Mum," Hamid says, pulling on the door handle to get out.

"And I have to be up at six!" Mrs Abdi calls after him. "So come in *quietly*, okay, Hamid?"

"Okay, okay!" Hamid says as he slams the car door. He looks up at the stark front of his aunt and uncle's house, and beyond it into the night sky. The moon is full tonight, and very bright. It'll be blocked by thick, grey clouds soon if the storm is as bad as the meteorologist is saying it will be.

As Hamid walks towards the front door, Aunt Julie comes outside and stands on the grey stone porch, waving. "Hi, Hamid!"

she says, chipper and smiling, her teeth as big and white as a sledging hill before the first run. She's wearing a gown that is long and shimmery and off-white, and it makes Hamid think of wintertime.

"Hi, Aunt Julie," he says, slipping past her and into the house.

As he steps inside, Julie peers up at the sky. "Not raining yet," she says. "They're saying we'll get a big storm tonight. I hope it can hold off till after we're home."

"I wouldn't mind a storm," Hamid says. "I like them."

"I don't usually mind them," Aunt Julie says, closing the door behind them, "but I don't think Mo wants to drive for two hours in a thunderstorm tonight."

Julie and Mo's house is huge and elegant, just as impressive inside as out – except for one odd thing. Julie is obsessed with clowns. And usually, clowns are everywhere.

But tonight, when Hamid walks in, he realizes that there is something different about the house. Tonight all the clown stuff is missing.

Normally there are photos of clowns on every shelf and framed drawings and paintings of clowns decorating the walls. There are usually countless porcelain miniature clowns that sit on the mantel above the fireplace in the family room.

Hamid peers around the corner to his left, down the short corridor that leads to the living room. There are usually stuffed clown dolls sitting in armchairs and clown music boxes and snow globes perched on every available table. No clowns.

Hamid turns to his right. The mirror that hangs on the wall over the half-circle table usually has antique postcards of clowns, both drawn and photographed, tucked under its frame. But not tonight.

Then Hamid looks up the staircase that leads to the dark second floor. Its walls are usually lined with black-and-white photos of clowns from a hundred years ago. Clowns performing in circuses, rodeos and street festivals. Clowns posing in random places you'd never think to find them – in a cafe, on the front porch of a house, in an open field.

"Aunt Julie," Hamid says slowly as he turns around to find her fiddling with something in the closet. "What happened to all your ... *stuff*?"

"It's all packed away, I'm afraid," Aunt Julie says quickly, turning to face him. She checks the time on her phone and mutters to herself, "We really have to go." Then she looks at Hamid, frowning.

"Why is it all packed?" Hamid asks.

Just then, without warning, Uncle Mo steps through the doorway from the living room and walks up to the mirror that hangs over the semicircular table.

"Because, Hamid," Uncle Mo says as he tugs and twists and pulls at his bow tie, "your Aunt Julie's obsession with clowns has become a thing of nightmares." His eyes find Hamid in the mirror, and he opens them wide and then winks.

"Nightmares?" Hamid says. He looks at Aunt Julie for a clue. Sometimes she acts as a translator for Uncle Mo, when he's not making much sense.

"Well," Julie says, pausing to hush her husband and holding her finger to her lips, "Afifa and Ahmed have been having bad dreams."

"About clowns," Uncle Mo says, leaning down to put his goofiest face right between Hamid and Julie. He stands up straight, takes a last look in the mirror, and says, "I'm going to start the car."

Julie rolls her eyes. "Anyway," she says, "we thought maybe if we took down my collection and packed it all up, it might help the twins."

"And?" Hamid says.

She frowns at him. "It hasn't helped yet," she admits, and she snatches her bag from the hallway table in front of the mirror. "Well, they're asleep for now."

"Not for long!" Mo calls from around the corner in the kitchen, probably on his way to the garage.

"All right, all right," Julie says. "We have to get going. But I'm afraid your uncle is right. The twins will probably be up at some point tonight with bad dreams." As she talks, she digs around in her little silver bag. "If they do get up," she says, "please just do your best to reassure them and get them back to bed. They like you and trust you, so it shouldn't be a problem."

"Okay," Hamid says.

"Meanwhile," Julie goes on, "you have the run of the house. There's food and fizzy drink in the fridge. And there's microwave popcorn. Do you know how to make microwave popcorn?"

"Of course," Hamid says, rolling his eyes a little.

"Of course," Julie says, still digging through her bag. "And there are lots of films to watch on cable or Blu-ray or whatever else Mo has hooked up in there. You know how to use that stuff?"

"Of course."

"Of course," Julie says, finally looking up from her bag. "Honey!" she calls out over her shoulder towards the kitchen. "I can't find the tickets."

"I have them in my coat pocket," Mo calls back, sticking his head around the corner. "Let's go!"

Aunt Julie shakes her head and smiles. "Anyway," she says, "if the twins get up, just let them know they're safe and get them back to bed, all right?"

"No problem," Hamid says, and he walks with Aunt Julie through the kitchen – gleaming stainless steel, granite worktops, and a rack of shining copper pots and pans over the island – to the garage. He peeks in and sees that Uncle Mo is already in the driver's seat of their sporty SUV, tapping his watch impatiently.

"Have a good time," Hamid says, waving at Mo, who waggles his tongue at him.

No wonder Julie loves clowns so much, Hamid thinks. *She's married to one.*

Julie smiles and waves and climbs into the car. "Call us if you need anything!" she says through the open window as Mo backs out of the garage. "My mobile number is on the fridge!"

Hamid steps back into the kitchen and closes the door. Then he pulls open the doors to the walk-in larder and rubs his hands together as he looks around. "Popcorn and film time," he says.

CHAPTER 2

The TV that Hamid and his mum have at home isn't terrible. It's big enough so that when Hamid watches football, he can usually tell which player has the ball. And if he turns the volume up loud enough during his favourite action films, he can feel the explosions right in his belly.

Of course, when he turns it up that loud, the neighbours usually complain. The flat's walls are paper thin, and with neighbours next to, below and above them, there's always someone who can hear it.

Aunt Julie and Uncle Mo's TV, though,

makes his own TV look like the portable black-and-white one his great-grandma keeps on her kitchen worktop. Julie and Mo's TV – with high-definition picture and a 3D setting – takes up most of one wall in their living room. Or it would anyway, if it was a normal wall.

Instead the ceiling in the living room is twice as high as any ceiling Hamid has ever seen. They also have a cable package, which has every premium film channel.

When you put it all together, Hamid doubts that Mo's family ever bothers going to the cinema. Why would they, with a set-up like this right here at home?

Hamid's hands are greasy from the buttery popcorn. He's watching a re-run of his favourite sitcom when the TV begins to beep and an alert scrolls across the bottom of the screen. The beeping drowns out the voices in his programme.

Then an automated voice comes on: "Severe thunderstorm warning in effect for Lincoln County, Brighton County, Kells County and the whole New Brighton metro area. High winds, heavy rain, thunder and lightning."

"Yeah, yeah," Hamid says. "I can't hear the programme!"

When the beeping finally stops and the alert goes away, the voices on his sitcom come back – just in time for a huge laugh. "Great," he mutters. "I probably missed the funniest line."

He leans back on the sofa as lightning flashes through the giant windows behind him. A few seconds later, the room shakes as thunder booms. An instant later, Hamid hears quick footsteps above him.

At first, he thinks maybe the sound came from the massive TV – the audio is so realistic, after all – so he mutes the programme and leans forward like a dog twitching her ears as the postman approaches.

The footsteps come again, heavy and slow this time. Hamid tosses the remote against the sofa cushions and hurries to the stairs. He peers up into the darkness, but he can't see a thing up there.

"Ahmed?" he calls. There's no answer.

"Afifa, is that you?" Hamid says. "Get back to bed."

Still no answer, but there are more heavy footsteps, moving quickly this time. Lightning flashes, lighting up the upstairs landing for a fraction of a second – long enough to see a hunched figure hurry away. Thunder booms as darkness falls over the landing once again.

"Ahmed," Hamid groans. He flicks the switch that turns on the lights upstairs. The light flashes for an instant and then goes out.

"Great," he mutters. "The bulb must have gone."

With a sigh, he climbs the stairs, though he's not thrilled about having to go up there with the lights still off. When he's halfway up, Hamid hears the click of a shutting door and grins.

"I can hear you!" he calls, taking the stairs two at a time. The second floor is nearly pitch black, and because Hamid isn't as familiar with it as he is with the first floor, he has to wait a moment while his eyes adjust to the darkness.

Soon lightning cracks and Hamid sees the outlines of doors near by. One is very close, right across the landing from the top of the stairs. The others are still hard to see, further down the landing.

In the darkness, he's not even sure which is the twins' room, so he goes to the first door, keeping his hand on the wall to guide him. When thunder crashes, he feels the wall vibrate.

At the first door, Hamid knocks gently. "Ahmed," he whispers loudly through the door. "Are you back in bed?"

He turns the doorknob quietly and slowly. He opens the door just a tiny bit, so he can peek in. But he can tell at once – this isn't the twins' room. Soft light from the old-fashioned-looking streetlamps on the road comes in through the rain-coated windows at the back of the room. It casts a watery amber light over the king-size bed in the middle of the room and the dressers and TV that face the bed. It's obviously his aunt and uncle's room.

He should just close the door and try the next one. But he can't help stepping inside to have a look around. It's so different from his mum's bedroom in their flat. Nicer, bigger furniture. Those huge windows. It even smells different.

Lightning cracks and thunder booms as Hamid takes a step towards the bed. The room lights up, and Hamid sees something that makes him scream out loud.

In a rocking chair beside the bed sits ... *a person? No, not a person,* Hamid realizes as he takes a closer look. *A life-size clown doll. Of course.*

"That thing is ridiculous," Hamid whispers to himself, forcing a smile. But his heart is racing and his breath is coming in shallow little gasps. He feels pretty silly, being scared of a doll.

"Looks like Aunt Julie didn't clear out *all* the clown stuff," he says as he catches his breath and his heart rate slows to normal.

It's a huge bedroom, and he notices that there's a bathroom attached. But he no longer feels like snooping around. He walks over to the rocking chair and kicks the clown doll in the foot.

"Stupid clown," he says, thinking the kick and the comment would help him feel less afraid. It doesn't work, though, because for an instant the clown seems to be looking right at him. It gives him a chill, and suddenly Hamid can't get out of the room quickly enough.

Hamid hurries to the bedroom door and pulls it shut behind him. More used to the darkness now, he moves down the landing. The next door he passes is ajar. Hamid peeks inside it and sees that it's the bathroom the twins use, complete with brightly coloured shampoo bottles and an animal-themed shower curtain. The next door – decorated with several art projects and miniature plastic licence plates that say AHMED and AFIFA – is the twins' bedroom. It's open a little, too.

"Are you two in bed?" he asks, poking the door so it opens just a little more and he can see inside.

"Hi, Cousin Hamid," Ahmed says. He's sitting up in bed with his torch, pointing it at his own face. "I thought I heard your voice. Who were you talking to?"

"Hi, Ahmed," Hamid says, ignoring the question. He isn't about to admit to his little cousins that he screamed because he was scared of a giant doll.

He sits on the edge of Ahmed's bed and takes the torch. "You need to get back to sleep," he says. Hamid switches off the torch and puts it down on the floor beside Ahmed's bed.

"Leave it on!" comes Afifa's squeaky voice from her bed on the other side of the room.

"You're awake, too?" Hamid says. He gets up and crosses to Afifa. She's also sitting up, propped against her pillows.

"Please leave the light on," she says, her voice a little whiny. "You have to."

"Why do I have to?" says Hamid.

"She's just scared," Ahmed says. He rolls onto his side and pulls the blanket over his head. "We had a bad dream." His voice is muffled from the thick blanket he's under. "I heard you shout, and I thought maybe you had the same bad dream."

"Shout?" Hamid repeats. "Oh, that. No, I just – something surprised me. It was silly." He sits on the edge of Afifa's bed. "Your mum said you've been having nightmares."

"We're not having nightmares," Afifa says. "Nightmares aren't real." She crosses her arms and lowers her chin.

Hamid can hardly see her eyes in the darkness, but it sounds like she's been crying.

"You think there's something mean and real in the house?" Hamid says. He moves closer to her and puts an arm around her shoulders. "Hey, come on, Afifa," he says. "You're a big girl. And you've got your brother, Ahmed, here and your big cousin Hamid just downstairs."

She looks up at him and sniffles.

"There's nothing here that can hurt you," Hamid says. "And besides, Ahmed and I will protect you. Okay?"

Afifa takes a moment to think it over. "Okay," she says, but she doesn't sound entirely convinced. He helps her settle back into bed and pulls the blanket over her again. As he's leaving, though, she sits up again.

"But Hamid," she says, "who will protect you and Ahmed?"

CHAPTER 3

Despite their nightmares, the twins can't stay awake even if they want to. Hamid is hardly out of the room before he hears Ahmed's gentle snoring and Afifa's cooing breath, slow and steady.

"Poor things," he mutters as he heads back downstairs. "They seem so scared."

The sitcom he'd been watching is long over by the time Hamid reaches the sofa and unmutes the TV. The next programme is one he doesn't like, so he switches to a film channel and finds a superhero film with lots of explosions.

"This'll do," he says to himself. He grabs a handful of popcorn and settles down to watch.

It's only a few minutes later that the TV begins to beep again, this time drowning out the soundtrack to an insane rocket-ship chase through the heart of a city on fire.

"We know!" Hamid shouts at the TV as the text crawl appears at the bottom of the screen. "There's a storm coming! It's already here!"

But the report isn't about a storm.

"Washington County authorities have released further information about escaped convict Josiah Pryce," comes the robotic voice. "It is now thought that Pryce may be heading for the city of New Brighton."

"Whoa," Hamid says. He leans forward and waits for more. Lightning cracks. Thunder shakes the house only an instant later. That one was very close.

The voice continues. "Pryce will probably be looking for–"

Suddenly, the TV switches off. The light in the hallway flickers and goes out.

"Um," Hamid says, sitting up straight to look around the dark living room. He turns to peer over the back of the sofa. The only light comes in through the huge windows behind him – huge windows without blinds that look out into the stormy back garden.

The windows run with the downpour, so the silvery glow of the garden security light flickers and bounces like it's part of the storm.

"The security light? Why is that on if the rest of the power is out?" Hamid wonders aloud.

Hamid moves towards the window. He looks out through the pouring rain into the soaked back garden, a sloping lawn leading up to a long, tall row of evergreen trees.

He lets his forehead rest against the window. "There's no one out there," he says. His breath fogs up the glass. "With that bright light on, I'd see them."

At that very moment, the security light turns off. Hamid jumps back from the window.

"I don't like this," he says to himself as he backs up to the sofa.

In his pocket, his phone vibrates. Hamid checks the number: it's his friend Malik.

"What's up?" Hamid says into the phone. "Have you guys lost power?"

"No," says Malik.

Hamid can hear whatever game they're playing in the background. It sounds like Kamaal is over there, too. Hamid can hear him shouting about the game.

"But did you hear about this man who escaped from prison?" Malik asks.

Hamid drops onto the sofa and stares at the dark TV screen. "Yeah," he says. "I heard about it on the radio earlier. And I just saw on TV that he might be heading towards the city."

"Are you freaked out?" Malik says. "We're pretty freaked out." He laughs.

"Nah," says Hamid as he leans back onto the sofa. "I'm not worried. That prison is over 160 kilometres away from here. Also my mum said the police will catch him in no time."

"Pff," says Malik. "What does your mum know about it?"

Hamid shrugs. "I'm not worried," he says, even though it's not entirely true. "Anyway, what game are you playing?"

"Oh man," Malik says. "It's sick." Malik goes on to tell Hamid all about the game – a full-on assault by aliens from one side and zombies from the other.

But Hamid is hardly listening. His eyes find the huge back windows again. And now, with the bright security light off, there really could be anyone out there.

Someone could be standing right at the window, watching him.

And Hamid would have no idea.

CHAPTER 4

Hamid is still talking – or listening – to Malik when lightning cracks and thunder booms again and the security light comes back on. The lights in the hallway turn on, and Hamid hears the TV come back on, too.

"Hey, the power's back on," he says, interrupting Malik's commentary on Kamaal's video-gaming session. "I'm gonna make some more popcorn." Hamid had finished his first bag a few minutes ago while Malik was talking.

"All right," says Malik. "Keep the doors locked!" He laughs as he hangs up.

Hamid crumples up the empty popcorn bag and heads for the kitchen, passing through the front hallway and the bottom of the stairs on the way. He's not feeling as afraid as he was a few minutes ago. Talking to his friend and getting the power back has helped him relax quite a bit. Still, he makes a point of not looking up the stairs into the darkness as he passes.

The kitchen is bright and still smells from the last bag of popcorn he microwaved. Hamid feels better straight away. He pulls open the larder door and reaches into the popcorn box, but he finds it empty. That was the last bag, apparently.

"Aw man," he says, feeling a little irritated with Aunt Julie and Uncle Mo for only having one bag of popcorn. "So what can I snack on now?" He steps further into the big larder and pokes around. No crisps. No fruit snacks. No sweets. No biscuits. It's the worst larder ever, full of tins of beans, short round tins of fish with labels in Russian, and vacuum-sealed packs of meat with writing in Spanish and Italian and French. None of it is anything Hamid wants to eat – or even knows *how* to eat.

Behind him, in the empty kitchen, the door squeaks.

Hamid hurries from the larder in time to see the swinging door to the front hallway flapping to a stop, as if someone has just walked through it.

"Ahmed?" he says. "Is that you?"

No reply.

Hamid doesn't want to think about the man who escaped from the prison north of the city. He doesn't want to imagine that man hitchhiking in the thunder and lightning, maybe even stealing a car, maybe even pulling a driver from a car and leaving the driver on the side of the road.

But he can't help it.

Hamid pushes through the kitchen door and stops at the bottom of the stairs. He peers up into the darkness but sees nothing.

He sticks his head through the doorway to the living room – lit only by the glow of the TV and the silvery light of the security light coming in through the windows. He expects to find his mischievous little cousins splayed out on the big sofa and watching a film they're definitely not supposed to be watching. But there's no one there.

The TV is beeping again and Hamid can hear the announcer's voice. The scroll at the bottom of the screen is nearly gone by the time Hamid hurries over. He catches the very end: ... *police say Pryce may be heading for the city's west end.*

West end? Hamid thinks. *That's here.*

CHAPTER 5

Upstairs, a door creaks. Hamid mutes the TV and calls towards the steps, "Afifa?"

A loud whisper comes back from upstairs. "Hamid!"

"Huh?" he says, tossing the remote control onto the sofa. He goes to the bottom of the steps and at the top, both in their jammies and looking down at him – Ahmed holding his torch and Afifa holding her stuffed stegosaurus – are his twin cousins.

"What are you two doing out of bed again?" he says as he climbs the stairs. "You scared me, running around like that."

Ahmed and Afifa look at each other for an instant, then back at Hamid.

"We had another nightmare," Ahmed says, his eyes wide.

"No we didn't," Afifa says.

Hamid gently puts a hand on each of their backs and leads them back down the landing. "If you didn't," he asks, "then why are you awake and out of bed?"

The twins stop at their bedroom door. Ahmed gives Afifa a gentle shove. "Tell him if you're gonna," he says.

She shakes her head. "I don't wanna."

Ahmed shrugs.

"Look," says Hamid. "It's late. I don't want to see you two out of bed again tonight. Do you understand?"

The twins nod.

"Good," he says as he pushes their bedroom door open. "Now go back to bed."

The twins reluctantly walk to their beds and climb under the covers.

"Won't you tuck us in again?" Afifa says.

"No way," says Hamid. "And stay in bed this time!"

He closes the door and heads for the steps, but stops short at his aunt and uncle's room. The door is open – just a crack – and he's sure he closed it earlier.

"That's weird," he says to himself. "The twins must be playing a joke on me."

He pokes his head through the door to the master bedroom. Everything seems as it was when he left it before, so he pulls the door shut and then checks to make certain it's truly closed. It sticks a little, but the knob clicks. It's definitely closed this time.

Hamid heads back to the kitchen and finds an old cereal bar, the kind with chocolate chips, at the back of the larder. It's the closest thing to a biscuit, so he grabs it and a carton of juice. When he finishes those, he closes his eyes.

He won't fall asleep. He just needs a little rest. He isn't used to staying up this late, after all. But soon he's pulled up his feet and dropped his head onto a throw pillow, and he's imagining he's in his bed at home.

* * *

Something wakes him. A voice, he thinks for a moment. *Mum?*

No. He's not at home. He's at Uncle Mo and Aunt Julie's house. He's babysitting. The twins are upstairs sleeping. Hamid is all alone.

But I swear I heard a voice, he thinks. *I guess it must've just been a dream.*

The living room is almost completely dark now. The film must have just ended, Hamid realizes, because the screen is black now, aside from the small white print of the end credits.

Hamid sits up, his head still foggy with dreams and sleep. He grabs the remote and presses the channel-change button. Anything would be better than a nearly black screen. He finds the late local news, with two smiling hosts, and the room feels safer straight away. It also shows the time at the bottom of the screen: 11.25.

"Wow," Hamid mutters, stretching. "I slept for a long time."

At least the twins are still asleep, he thinks as he stands up to stretch again and head to the kitchen. Maybe he missed a box of biscuits in that huge larder. He should check the freezer.

But he doesn't make it to the kitchen before he hears a deafening, blood-curdling shriek from upstairs.

CHAPTER 6

"Afifa? Ahmed?" Hamid shouts, running for the stairs. He takes them two at a time and slams open the twins' door. "What happened?"

Afifa and Ahmed stand next to each other on Ahmed's bed, his torch beam fixed on the open door. Hamid shields his eyes from the bright light. "Shut that thing off!" he snaps.

Ahmed points the beam at his own face instead.

Then Hamid asks, "What's going on? Are you two okay?"

He sees Ahmed nod in the glow from the torch and continues, "What's a boy your age doing with a torch that bright anyway? Are you a police officer on patrol or something?" Hamid sighs. "Both of you sit down," he says as he walks over to the bed.

The twins sit on their beds and look up at him.

"Why don't you tell me what's going on?" Hamid says.

"Nightmares," Ahmed says. He shoots his sister a glance.

"Nope," she says.

"Then tell him," Ahmed whispers angrily, "if you want to."

"I don't want to," Afifa says.

"Then I'll tell him," Ahmed says.

"If you want to," Afifa says with a shrug.

"Tell me what?!" Hamid explodes.

"About the nightmare," Ahmed says.

"It's not a nightmare," Afifa insists.

"I think it is," Ahmed says. He looks at Hamid. "We have the same nightmare."

Hamid feels his spine tingle. "Really?" he says. "That's weird, isn't it?"

"It's because we're twins," Ahmed says.

"No, it isn't," Afifa says.

Ahmed nods. "It is," he says. "I read that on the internet. Twins have special mental powers."

"What websites have you been visiting?" Hamid asks.

Ahmed shrugs.

"Well, tell me about it," Hamid says. "Tell me about your bad dream."

The only light in the room comes in through the slim gap between the shade and the windowsill. It's silver moonlight and golden light coming from the streetlamp in front of the house. The only sound in the room is Afifa's rushed breath – anxious and shallow.

"It always starts the same," Ahmed says, leaning forward a little, his big eyes growing even wider. "Me and Afifa are in bed – she's in hers and I'm in mine – and it's night-time, just like it is right now."

Hamid's heart starts beating faster. It's silly, he knows, but Ahmed's childish voice and frightened tone are giving him the shivers. Maybe he's already on edge because of the escaped convict on the loose – maybe near by.

Ahmed points the torch at Hamid and then points it back at his own face and continues. "I always say to Afifa, 'Are you awake?' And she whispers back, 'Yes. And so are you'."

"Because he is," Afifa adds.

"Then the doorknob clicks," Ahmed goes on, ignoring his sister, "and the hinges creak and squeak, and slowly, slowly, slowly the door begins to open."

"And it's dark on the landing," Afifa says. "It's always dark out there. It's never when the landing light is on."

"Never," Ahmed says. "The light is never on. But it doesn't matter, because we don't have to see it. We know what's there."

Ahmed takes his sister's hand and they look at each other and say, "The clown."

Hamid nods. Of course it's a clown. Like Aunt Julie said – that's why she put away all the clown decorations, apart from that life-size doll in her bedroom.

I wonder if the twins know it's still there, Hamid thinks.

"Listen," he says, keeping his voice gentle and bringing a soothing smile to his face – at least he hopes it's soothing. "The clowns that your mum collects, they can't hurt you. You know that, right?"

"Yes, we know," Afifa replies. "Of course we know."

Hamid is relieved about that much, at least.

Ahmed nods. "*Mummy's* clowns aren't real," he says, and his voice is flat and cold.

Hamid decides then and there to ask his aunt about the clown in the bedroom. Ahmed and Afifa are obviously still upset. Maybe it's time to say goodbye to the biggest and worst of the bunch.

"So what does he do?" Hamid asks. "The clown man who comes into your bedroom, I mean."

Ahmed glances at Afifa. It's as if they've spoken without speaking – like they can send messages to one another with just their minds. Afifa takes a deep breath and continues for Ahmed.

"He's bigger than me and Ahmed," Afifa says, her voice a timid whisper, nothing like the loud whisper Hamid heard from upstairs earlier tonight.

But what if that wasn't her? he wonders.

The idea leaves Hamid feeling cold. He grips the edge of Ahmed's blanket like he would have gripped his little stuffed dog when he was their age.

"He's as big as you, Cousin Hamid," she says. "And he tiptoes into the room till he's between our beds. And then he just stands there, staring at us and grinning."

"Like a clown," Ahmed says, his voice trembling.

"Does he hurt you?" Hamid says.

Afifa shakes her head. "He just smiles," she says. "Then he steps closer and closer, like he wants to tell us something. The first time it happened, we just smiled back at him."

"But then his smile..." Ahmed says, but he trails off.

Afifa finishes for him in a whisper: "He looks creepy."

"Mean," Ahmed adds.

"It makes me cry," Afifa says. "And I always scream when he starts to come closer to one of us. So then he runs out."

"And that wakes me up," says Ahmed.

"You're awake the whole time!" Afifa insists.

Could she really, truly believe that this evil clown is visiting their bedroom at night? Hamid wonders.

But then a little voice in his head whispers, *Do I believe it, too?*

He checks the clock. It's nearly midnight now, and he's exhausted. "It sounds like a very scary dream," he says. He scoops up Afifa in his arms and lays her back on her own bed. "But you really need to get back to sleep."

"All right, Cousin Hamid," Afifa says.

"Good night," Hamid says as he walks out of the room. "And this time, stay in bed!"

CHAPTER 7

Hamid is back on the living room sofa. It is just after midnight now, and he's watching a late-night comedy programme that he has never seen before. Hamid has been up this late a few times, usually at Malik's house or on New Year's Eve. Those times, though, Hamid had been watching a film or playing a video game with his friends or watching New Year celebrations with his mum.

"I don't get it," he mutters. Half the programme's cast is in a living room set and dressed as chickens. It's the weirdest thing he's ever seen, but it's not exactly funny. He'd hoped it would make him laugh to chase away the anxiety he's been trying to control since his little cousins told him about their nightmare.

But it's not making him laugh. In fact, it's not even a decent distraction. Instead, all he can think about is the windows behind him and the storm and the giant clown doll in his aunt and uncle's bedroom, with its painted-on grin and the thick white face paint surrounding its beady eyes.

It looked *right at him.*

Still trying to distract himself, Hamid flips through the channels, the numbers getting higher, but he doesn't find anything worth watching. He yawns. He's feeling tired again.

Hamid lets his head fall back against the super-cushiony pillows on the sofa. He closes his eyes, and in an instant, he's asleep and dreaming.

* * *

Hamid's dream is the kind of dream that seems to start before you even fall asleep. He gets up from the sofa. He hears Afifa whisper his name from just outside the living room.

"Afifa?" he whispers back. He has to be quiet. Someone is looking for him.

Who's looking for him? He can't remember. But he knows someone is. He's sure of it.

Afifa whispers again.

This time it's coming from the kitchen. The light is on in there, and Hamid pushes through the swinging door. But as he does so, lightning flashes and thunder crashes. The door doesn't lead to the kitchen. It leads to Aunt Julie and Uncle Mo's bedroom, which is almost pitch black.

He stumbles on something and has to lean on the wall to stop himself from falling. The wall is cold and wet, like it's made of ice.

The chill against his hand runs up his arm and down his back. He shivers.

The clown doll is just where it was before, seated in the rocking chair. But the chair is moving now, rocking gently, as if someone has given it a shove and then walked away.

The clown's painted-on smile stretches and twists and splits. It begins to laugh – quietly at first, like a stifled giggle. But then it bubbles and squeaks and explodes into a goofy, mad cackle.

Hamid backs up and reaches for the door behind him, but it's closed now – locked, actually.

He shakes the knob and hears his twin cousins just outside the door.

Afifa shouts, "You're awake, Cousin!"

Ahmed shouts, "It's a dream, Cousin!"

"Please," he screams through the door. "Open the door! Let me out!"

He looks over his shoulder and sees the clown doll slowly rising from the chair, still laughing its nasty laugh.

Hamid pounds on the door. "Open the door!" he shouts as loud as he can.

The clown reaches out its hands for him – dirty gloves, once white, in front of the cackling, painted face. Hamid presses himself against the locked door as the clown comes closer and closer.

The monstrous doll laughs and laughs. Its cackle is raspy and thin and endless.

It almost sounds like...

A phone ringing.

Hamid wakes and sits up with a start. He feels hot, but icy sweat drips down his forehead and the middle of his back.

And his phone is ringing.

The dream is already jumbled in his mind, and Hamid can hardly remember the details at all. He only knows he was more afraid than he's ever been.

He fumbles around for his phone on the coffee table as it keeps ringing. "Who calls this late?" he says to himself, but then he realizes it must be Aunt Julie calling to check in. He grabs the phone, though he's a bit breathless and can hear his heart beating fast in his ears. "Hello?" he says, as he reaches for the remote to mute the TV.

"Ah, Hamid," says Julie. There's lots of noise in the background – people talking loudly, music playing, the clinking of glasses and plates. "I hope you've been able to stay awake."

"Hi, Aunt Julie," says Hamid. He can't tell her that he fell asleep. "I'm hanging in there so far."

"Good," she says. "We're finally getting ready to leave. The speeches were *so long*, and the whole dinner ran late."

"It's no problem," Hamid says. *What time is it, anyway?* he wonders.

"Good," says his aunt. "I'm afraid the drive will take forty-five minutes or so."

"That's okay," Hamid says.

It's not okay, actually – that's what he'd like to say. He'd like his aunt and uncle to walk in the front door right now. He just wants to get out of this house. He wants to be safe at home. And that clown in Aunt Julie and Uncle Mo's bedroom? He wishes they would get rid of it.

"As I have you on the phone, Aunt Julie..." Hamid begins.

"Yes?" she says.

"Well, it's about Ahmed and Afifa," Hamid says, sitting up. "You know how they've been having nightmares lately?"

"Oh no," Aunt Julie says. "They haven't been out of bed a lot, have they?"

"A couple of times, yes," says Hamid. "But that's not what I wanted to tell you. I wanted to tell you about the cl–"

"Just a minute, Hamid," Aunt Julie says. "I can hardly hear you in this madhouse. Mohammed is getting our coats. The queue at the cloakroom is so long. I've never seen such crowds!"

The phone is muffled for a moment. Hamid can hear voices, but he can't make out Aunt Julie's voice – if she's saying anything.

"Hello?" he says, covering his other ear. "Aunt Julie, are you still there?"

"Sorry," she says. "I got bumped in the crowd a bit. I'll head out front where I can hear you better. Don't go anywhere."

The line goes quiet, but they are still connected. Aunt Julie must have tapped the hold button. Hamid sags back on the sofa, holding the phone to his ear. He taps his fingers on his knee and stares at the TV screen, which is showing an advert.

It would be nice if the police could pick up that escaped convict, Hamid thinks. He clicks the TV over to the news channel, hoping for an update, but it looks like they're just doing business news.

The money news host is sitting there, grinning as he talks and gesturing wildly with his hands. It's actually funny, muted like this, and Hamid almost laughs.

"Come on, Aunt Julie," he says. "How long can it take to walk out of a building?"

He picks up the remote and flips through the channels. A comedy programme, local news, business news, sports highlights, an old film, another old film...

But then he jumps as hurried footsteps thump on the floor above him.

Hamid tosses the remote as he stands and moves towards the front hallway to check on the noise. Obviously Ahmed and Afifa have had another nightmare. It makes him remember his nightmare a little.

The image of that clown doll flashes into his mind. But in the image it's smiling – and standing.

As Hamid makes his way towards the stairs, Aunt Julie's voice gasps into his ear, startling him.

"Sorry about that, Hamid," she says, breathless. "You wouldn't believe how huge this place is – and how crowded. It took me all that time to push through the madness and find the exit."

She catches her breath and lets out a big, dramatic sigh. "So, you were saying? About the twins?"

"I sat down with them," Hamid says. He turns in the doorway to face the living room again and its huge windows. The security light is off again, though the power is obviously on in the rest of the house. The windows are covered in black sheets of rain.

If someone were out there right now, he wouldn't be able to tell.

"Afifa and Ahmed told me all about the nightmare they've been having," Hamid says. "Afifa is so scared of this nightmare that she doesn't even believe it's a dream. She thinks it's really happening. She thinks she's really in danger."

Julie clucks a sad little sound. "I know," she says. "I feel terrible about it. And to think it might be because of my clown art collection. It's so upsetting."

"Maybe you should get all of it put away, then," Hamid says.

More footsteps come from upstairs, this time heavy and slow, like an elephant is charging across the landing.

"Hold on a second," Hamid says. He takes the phone from his ear and turns his back on the living room. He steps into the front hall and out of the corner of his eye, he catches movement on the upstairs landing.

Hamid quickly says into the phone, "Just a second, Aunt Julie. I think the twins are awake again."

He covers the phone's mouthpiece and calls up the stairs, "Is that you, Ahmed?"

"Is he out of bed *again*?" Aunt Julie says. Her voice sounds faraway, with the earpiece away from his head. She groans. "He's going to be exhausted tomorrow."

Hamid peers up the stairs into the darkness. If Ahmed had been there, he isn't there anymore – or he's lurking in the shadows. But that doesn't sound like something Ahmed would do.

"I thought I saw him up there, but he's not there now," Hamid says as he brings the phone back to his ear. "I must have been imagining it."

Hamid shakes his head. *Why am I so scared?* he wonders. *The twins are seven years old. I'm fourteen. I should know that a fake clown – even one as big as me – is nothing to be afraid of.*

"I suppose that nightmare of theirs has me a little spooked, too," he admits to Aunt Julie. "Or maybe it's the criminal on the loose," he adds, but she doesn't seem to be listening.

She's talking over him. "What were you about to say, Hamid?" she says. "Something about putting away the clowns? I have put away the clowns."

Hamid hears Uncle Mo in the background and Julie's voice, muffled and away from the phone. "It's Hamid," she tells Mo. "He says the twins have been up a lot with that bad dream again."

Hamid moves through to the kitchen. Standing at the bottom of the stairs felt too creepy. The darkness – and the nightmare and the creepy rocking-chair clown – seems to whisper down to him. Even with his back to the stairs, he can feel the chill on his neck.

The kitchen is clean and white and lit up. It has no giant windows that an escaped convict might peek through.

"Let me talk to him," Mo says. "Hamid, my revered nephew! Are you having a rough time with the rug rats tonight? Have they been crawling on the ceilings and eating insects again?"

"Hi, Uncle Mo," Hamid says. "I was just telling Aunt Julie, Ahmed and Afifa told me all about their nightmare. It seems like they're really scared of that big clown."

"Big clown?" Mo says. Then, his voice a little muffled, "Hey, Jules. Do you have a big clown?"

"They said their nightmare is a big clown

coming into their room and watching them sleep," Hamid says as Julie comes back to the phone.

"A giant clown?" she says. "I don't have a giant clown. I mean, I have a rag doll, but it's only 30 centimetres tall. It's packed away with everything else."

Hamid's skin tingles. The hairs on the back of his neck go stiff. He manages a light laugh.

"I think you're forgetting one, Aunt Julie," he says as he paces from the kitchen to the hallway. "What about the one in your bedroom?"

As the words leave his mouth, Hamid realizes Aunt Julie and Uncle Mo probably wouldn't be happy to learn he'd been snooping around in their bedroom.

Mum has had a rule about no children in her bedroom forever, Hamid thinks. *Of course her brother's house would have the same rule.*

And now I just accidentally confessed to breaking it – all because of that silly clown.

"In our bedroom?" Aunt Julie says. She sounds shocked. Confused.

Hamid's face gets hot. "I didn't mean to go snooping, Aunt Julie. It was dark up there, and I didn't even know which room was the twins'. I just opened the first door I came to, and–"

"What?" Julie interrupts. "No, Hamid. I don't care that you went into our bedroom."

"Oh," Hamid says. "Then, what?"

"You said a big clown doll?" Julie says, laughing a little. "Like I said, the biggest clown doll I have is a rag doll that used to lie on my pillow. But you said you saw a big one on our rocking chair?"

"Yeah," Hamid says. "It's as big as me, even – sitting in the rocking chair in your bedroom." He shivers even as he says the words. "Creepiest thing I've ever seen."

"Mo," Aunt Julie says with the phone away from her mouth a little, "did you buy me a new clown doll? A big one? You know the children are afraid of clowns now!"

"I didn't buy anything..." Mo says in the background.

After that, there's silence.

"Aunt Julie?" Hamid says. He checks the phone to make sure they're still connected. "Aunt Julie, are you still there?"

"Hamid." It's Mo now. His voice is urgent. "Are you certain you saw a giant doll in our room?"

"Yes," Hamid says. "A big clown. Sitting in the rocking chair."

"Hamid, you need to get out of the house right now," says Mo. "You have to get the twins and get out of the house right now. Do you understand?"

Hamid's heart seems to skip a beat or two, then thumps hard against his ribs. His mouth goes dry. "Mo, what are you talking about?" he asks. "What's going on?"

Upstairs, the footsteps thump again, like they're running down the landing towards the stairs. Hamid makes his way over to the stairs and peers up into the darkness. "I think Ahmed is up again," Hamid says.

"Hamid, listen to me," Mo says. "Julie doesn't have a giant clown doll."

"Yes she does," Hamid says. "The one in the rocking chair." He starts up the stairs, holding his phone to his ear. Their connection crackles a little.

"She doesn't, Hamid," Mo says. "That's not a doll. There's someone in the house, Hamid. I'm calling the police. You and the twins have to get out of there."

CHAPTER 8

The footsteps on the landing upstairs ... those aren't Ahmed. They aren't Afifa.

They're him – the clown. The giant doll in Aunt Julie's rocking chair.

The man who escaped from prison, Hamid thinks as his heart pounds in his chest and his pulse races in his ears. *It's him. He's here. Why is he here?*

Hamid drops his phone. It bounces down the carpeted steps as Uncle Mo's voice says over and over, sounding further and further away, "Hamid, can you hear me? Hamid, get out of the house!"

He doesn't want to go upstairs. The clown is upstairs – the criminal is upstairs.

Hamid realizes he doesn't even know what the man was in prison for. *Is he a bank robber? A car thief?*

A murderer?

But he has to go upstairs, because the twins are upstairs, too. They might be asleep in their room. He might be in their room right now, standing in between their beds, watching them, waiting for Afifa to scream. But what if he's quiet this time? What if she never screams?

What if he's a kidnapper?

Hamid could tiptoe. He could be totally silent, creeping up the stairs and along the dark landing to the third door. The clown might not hear him.

Hamid braces himself against the wall. The wall feels cold – it reminds him of his dream.

In his dream, the clown came to life. He must have known. Somehow, deep down, he must have known while he slept that the clown was no doll – that it was actually a dangerous man.

Hamid moves slowly up the stairs. They creak under each slow footfall. From above, he hears the squeak of a doorknob and the creak of a door opening slowly.

He stops and holds his breath. He squints up and sees the door to Julie and Mo's bedroom. It's open, just a little – enough so the amber light coming in through the big windows pours out across the landing – and Hamid imagines the clown lurking just inside the door, hidden in the shadows, grinning madly, his beady eyes circled in white make-up, just waiting for Hamid to try to sneak by.

Light flashes in the open doorway – a lightning strike. A moment later, the house shakes with thunder. The storm is terrifying now – more violent than it's been all night. Hamid hears the drumming of heavy raindrops on the roof and windows.

He's nearly at the top now. He can see all the way along the landing. The door to the twins' room is closed tight.

What if he's in there? Hamid thinks. *What if he's not letting Afifa scream for help? He could have his gloved hand over her mouth.*

He can't wait any longer. Hamid leaps up the last two stairs onto the dark landing and sprints to the twins' room. He throws open the door, and Ahmed and Afifa sit up with a start. Ahmed clicks on the torch.

"Cousin Hamid?" Afifa says. "I didn't think it would be you."

"I know," Hamid says.

Should he tell them the truth? That the nightmares are real? That right at this moment there is a real stranger in the house, hiding just off the landing?

Afifa already knows the truth.

Still, Hamid can't bring himself to say it out loud. Maybe he doesn't want to believe it either. "The bad dreams are over now," he says. "I promise."

He puts out his hands to the children, inviting them to each take one and follow him. "We have to go outside," he says. "Who's your favourite neighbour?"

"Tucker!" Ahmed says, jumping up and down on his bed.

"Tucker lives three kilometres away," Afifa says. "We should go to Catherine's house."

"Aw, she's boring," Ahmed says.

"It doesn't matter," Hamid says as the twins take his hands. "Is she near by?"

"Just over the road," Afifa says.

"Perfect," says Hamid.

"Why do we have to go there?" Ahmed says. "Is this still part of the nightmare?"

"Yes," says Hamid. He stands with the twins in the doorway of their room and sticks his head out to check the landing. "This is the end of the nightmare."

"Are we awake right now?" Afifa asks.

Hamid can't answer. Instead he gives each little hand a squeeze. "Are you ready to run?" he asks.

The twins nod. Hamid counts in a whisper, "One, two, *three*," and they all run hand-in-hand for the stairs.

CHAPTER 9

They can't be silent. Little children's footsteps are always loud. They're even louder when they run.

The three of them are as loud as a herd of baby elephants running down the landing. At the top of the steps, Hamid stops. It's too narrow for the three of them to go down holding hands.

"Hurry down," he says, giving the twins each a light shove on the back. "Go outside."

From behind him, from beyond the slightly open door to Julie and Mo's bedroom, comes a goofy cackle and a jovial *honk, honk.*

Hamid slips on the top step and grabs the banister to stop himself falling and tumbling into the twins. He climbs to his feet again as the bedroom door behind him creaks. Hamid looks over his shoulder, both hands tight on the banister, and sees a white-gloved hand with long, dirty fingers wrapped around the door, opening it wider and wider.

"Go!" Hamid snaps at the twins, who have stopped at the bottom to wait for him. "Get out and run across the street!"

The laughing behind him grows louder. It's not goofy anymore. Now it's high-pitched and hysterical and crazed – just like the twins said it was.

Hamid is down the stairs before the twins have managed to get the front door open. It's too heavy and the handle too big and slippery for their little fingers. As Hamid grabs the handle, someone pounds on the door.

"Is anyone in there?" says a man. He has a booming voice, and he's shouting over the din of the storm.

The police, Hamid thinks. *They got here quickly.*

He pulls open the door. The wind rises and whips into the doorway, bringing with it sheets of rain. The drops hit Hamid's face like tiny pinpricks.

Standing in the doorway is a man. He towers over Hamid and the twins. His face is stern and square, with the shadow of a beard. He's not wearing a police officer's uniform, though.

"Did my uncle call you?" Hamid asks. He steps between the twins and the man.

"Of course," the man says. He steps further inside, out of the storm, and moves to close the door. "Who else would have called me?"

He smiles down at Hamid and the children, but it's a tight smile – an angry smile. "Now then," the man says. He's not shouting now. His voice is calm and cold. Rainwater runs down his cheeks like sweat on a cold drink. "I hear you have a visitor tonight?" he asks. He smiles even more, showing his teeth. They're yellowed. A couple of them are missing. A couple are chipped.

Hamid backs up with an arm around each twin. They back up with him. He thinks about the clown – still at the top of the stairs, maybe. Maybe standing there watching them.

He thinks about the twins' nightmares. They weren't nightmares at all, obviously.

But they started last week, he realizes. *The prison break was today*. He takes another step back, taking the twins with him. *So the clown can't be the escaped convict.*

"Who are you?" Hamid asks. He's backed up with the twins now all the way to the kitchen door.

The man with the square, unshaved jaw reaches up and loosens the collar of his shirt. "Who do you think I am?" he asks, and he's still grinning. Somehow this man's grin is even creepier to Hamid than the painted-on smile of that nightmare clown.

Hamid has an idea. This man is tired. He looks exhausted. He hasn't shaved. His collar is dirty and stained with sweat. His hands have a lot of fresh-looking scrapes. This is a man who's had a long, hard day.

And now he is here, in Hamid's aunt and uncle's house, dripping on their wood floors and grinning like the wolf that ate Grandma. He's here on the west side of New Brighton.

Just like the police said he would be.

But Hamid can't answer. Now that he knows who this man is, his voice is gone.

He doesn't need to speak, though, because a voice shrieks from the top of the stairs. It says just what Hamid would have said if he hadn't been too afraid to answer, "Pryce!"

Hamid and the twins turn and find the clown – the nightmare clown – standing above them.

The clown's face now isn't terrifying or evil. Instead it's full of fear. The same fear Hamid has in his chest, only much greater.

"How did you find me?" the clown screams. His gloved hand holds the stair railing as if he would collapse without its help. "How could you have found me?"

So it *is* Pryce. The escaped criminal. And he's here. All Hamid's horrible fears from the whole night have come true.

And now Pryce is standing between Hamid and the front door.

"I got myself a police scanner," Pryce says. He smiles up into the darkness. The clown watches him like he might watch a stray dog he's not sure is friendly.

"Someone," Pryce says as he eyes Hamid for just a second, "reported a home intruder dressed as a clown. Tell me, you madman, who else would do something this crazy?"

"Through the kitchen," Hamid whispers to the twins as Pryce takes a menacing step towards the stairs. "Quickly."

"I've been waiting for this moment for almost ten years," Pryce says. "And now I'll have my revenge."

Hamid and the twins push through the swinging door into the kitchen. "The garage," Hamid says. "Hurry."

The twins are sobbing now, holding Hamid's wrists with both hands, letting him drag them through their gleaming kitchen. He opens the garage door. The smell of tyres and motor oil nips at his nostrils.

Hamid quickly finds the glowing orange button near the door and slaps it as he pulls the twins through the garage.

The big metal door groans and screeches as it opens. It shakes and strains.

The blowing storm sends tiny daggers and darts of ice-cold rain into the garage. Afifa shrieks against the weather, and Ahmed throws his arm across his face.

Hamid ushers the twins into the driveway and across the wet grass, directly towards Catherine's house over the road. His socks are soaked in an instant, but he doesn't care. It's pouring anyway. Ahmed and Afifa, both barefoot and in their pajamas, flinch at the cold, wet ground and lift their shoulders against the downpour.

Blue and red lights flash up and down the street. When Hamid and the twins reach the kerb, at the same time that two police cars pull up, the twins are crying.

Everything is going to be okay, Hamid tells himself. *The police will take care of it all now.*

He turns to watch as the officers approach the house slowly. Hamid looks up at the middle window on the second floor – the biggest window on the front of the house. And there, behind the glass, are two figures. As Hamid watches, he sees a big man with a square jaw facing off with another man, stooped and afraid, with crazy hair at puffs on the sides of his head and a big, round nose.

CHAPTER 10

It is much later now, and Hamid and the twins are cuddling together on Catherine's sofa. It's a big fluffy sofa in a room covered in rugs, blankets and knitted throws. Hamid can see three cats from where he's sitting, and they are all very interested in the soaking wet trio that has shown up in the middle of the night to wake up their owner.

Though her house is as big as Julie and Mo's, and was probably once a very impressive house, now it's dusty and cluttered. Catherine seems to spend most of her time here in the front living room, with her cats and her knitting and her thick paperback novels that are piled in high stacks on every surface and fill every shelf in the room.

"You three have had quite a night," says Catherine. She sits in the stiff wooden chair next to the sofa. It's the only surface in the room not covered by a blanket, a doily or yarn. The moment she sits, a cat is on her knees. She pets it and smiles at Hamid.

Hamid can only nod. From where he sits in the centre of the sagging sofa, if he looks past a collection of wild-looking houseplants, he can see through Catherine's front window.

The police car lights still flash red and blue, sending twirling beams through the downpour and over the lawns and into the living rooms of his aunt and uncle's neighbours.

Catherine talks on and on about the last time the street saw this much excitement – she was much younger then, of course, and didn't have as many cats – but Hamid isn't really listening. He's looking out into the rainy middle of the night, waiting for word from Julie and Mo, the police or his mum that everything is okay and that everyone is safe now.

"Looks like it was too much for Ahmed and Afifa," Catherine says.

Hamid has a twin on either side of him, pressed against his ribs and tucked under his arms. They're both asleep now. He smiles a little, looking down at Afifa, who can sleep now knowing for certain that the clown won't walk in to watch her, and at Ahmed, who really is asleep, not just convincing himself he's asleep because reality has become too strange, too frightening.

There's some loud thumping at Catherine's front door, and then some more.

"That must be the police or your aunt and uncle," Catherine says, the small smile still on her lips. She lifts the cat from her lap as she stands and lets it perch on her shoulder. "Wait here."

Hamid lets his head fall back. *They've caught them. Finally,* he thinks.

When Aunt Julie and Uncle Mo come into the living room, both of them with panicked faces, streaked with a mixture of rainwater and tears, Hamid smiles up at them.

The police must have caught them, Hamid thinks.

He gives each cousin a little squeeze, not enough to wake them, and waits for his aunt or uncle to speak – to give him the good news that will let him sleep tonight.

But soon Hamid realizes that Aunt Julie is not smiling. She looks worried. She crouches in front the sofa and puts a hand on Hamid's knee. Her eyes are wet.

Uncle Mo stands behind her with a hand on her shoulder. "Hamid," he says, his voice as serious as Hamid's ever heard it. It has none of the playfulness it usually has. "Josiah Pryce is back in custody," he says. But Uncle Mo doesn't look relieved. "They found him in our kitchen," he says. "He was hiding there, cowering in the corner."

"Good," Hamid says. "Then why do you seem upset? We're okay. The twins are okay."

Mo sighs. He looks at his wife for a moment and then back at Hamid. "He wasn't wearing a clown costume, Hamid," he says.

"No," Hamid says, shaking his head. "Pryce wasn't the clown. He was going *after* the clown. Looking for him. The clown was afraid of him."

"The police looked all over the house," Mo goes on. He lowers his chin. His face grows darker. "They didn't find a man in a clown costume, Hamid."

"He probably ran off," Hamid says. "He was really afraid of Pryce. More afraid than we were, even."

Mo shakes his head. "There were no open doors or windows," he says. "There's no sign anyone else was there."

"Fingerprints!" Hamid offers, but the moment it's out of his mouth, he knows it won't work because the clown had been wearing gloves.

"They've been looking all over the property for the past hour," Mo went on. "They searched for any sign of him. They didn't find anything."

Hamid watches his aunt and uncle's faces. They don't change – they're both worried, confused and concerned.

"I don't understand," Hamid says. "He must be hiding in the house somewhere.

Did you tell the police he looks like a giant clown doll? He could be right back where he was in that rocking chair, and they wouldn't even know he wasn't a doll. I certainly didn't. Neither did the twins."

"We told them exactly what you told us on the phone," Julie says, patting Hamid's knee. She looks up at Mo for a long moment, then turns back to Hamid and adds, "They think you made it up."

"*Did* you make it up?" Mo asks, his face and voice are stern now.

"Of course not!" Hamid says. His voice is loud enough now that Ahmed wakes up for an instant and presses against his side, stretching.

Ahmed looks bleary-eyed as he glances up at his mum.

"Hi, sweetie," Julie says, finally smiling, though it's a sad and tired smile. "You had a scary night, huh?"

Ahmed nods. "Mmhmm," he says. "The clown came to life again. And there was a mean man in the house. But Cousin Hamid saved us."

"That's good, Ahmed," Julie says. She looks at Hamid now. "It's a good thing you have such a brave cousin, isn't it?"

Ahmed nods again. He lets his head fall against Hamid, and in a moment, he's asleep.

"See?" Hamid whispers. "Ahmed and Afifa will tell you. They saw the clown. They know he's real."

Mo sighs and squeezes Julie's shoulder.

"The twins have been having nightmares for a week, Hamid," Julie says, her voice even and calm, as if she's trying to soothe a panicked child or a wild animal. "Are we supposed to believe there's been a strange man dressed as a clown in our house for a *week*, and we just never noticed?"

Hamid doesn't know what to say. It does sound unbelievable. But he's sure of what he saw.

"We have to get the twins to bed," Mo says. "I'll drive you home, Hamid."

"What about the police?" Hamid asks as Aunt Julie stoops down to pick up Afifa. "They think I lied to them. Am I going to get into trouble?"

Mo sighs. "I've already talked to them," he says. "I think they've forgiven you, considering you also got Pryce for them. Besides, I think we're all convinced you at least believe you saw what you say you saw."

Hamid stands to let Mo scoop up Ahmed. "I did," Hamid says, but his voice is meek and unsure. "At least I think I did."

CHAPTER 11

On the journey home with Uncle Mo, Hamid goes over everything that happened earlier in his head.

It was a mostly normal night, really – until he told Julie and Mo about the giant clown doll in their bedroom. Why would he invent something like that? It doesn't make any sense.

"Listen, Hamid," Mo says. He keeps both hands on the steering wheel, gripping it tightly as they drive through the wet and windy night. "Do you think it's possible you made a mistake?"

"What do you mean?" Hamid asks. He looks across the front seat at his uncle as a bolt of lightning flashes up ahead.

"Like maybe you imagined it," Mo says. He keeps his eyes on the road. It's a bad night for driving. "This was a pretty crazy night, after all."

Hamid thinks for a moment. It's occurred to him already, of course, that he imagined the clown. He'd been so scared most of the night. When Pryce burst in, maybe he got overwhelmed and confused. Who knows what people will come up with when they're exhausted and terrified?

But no. He's sure. The clown spoke to Pryce. And what's more, Pryce spoke back.

"I didn't imagine it," Hamid says. He can hear the edge in his voice, but he's too tired to care.

"All right, all right," Mo says. "Hey, Ahmed and Afifa told you about their nightmare.

Maybe you fell asleep and dreamed about that doll in Julie's old rocking chair, huh? Maybe it snowballed together with Pryce."

Just like Hamid had been thinking.

"No," Hamid says. "I saw the doll before they told me about the dream. It was there."

He stares out over the wet roads as they get closer to Hamid's block of flats on the edge of the city. "And anyway," he adds quickly, "Afifa never said it was a dream. She kept saying they were awake – they were awake when the clown came in."

Mo glances at Hamid quickly and twists his mouth. "She's seven, Hamid," he says. "Her imagination is richer than yours and mine put together."

They are driving out of the city now. The buildings get smaller as they go, and the streets get a bit wider and bumpier. The pavements here are cracked and weedy, and the houses and blocks of flats are dirty and poorly cared for. The fresh rain and darkness make them look their best. In the morning, they will look sad and broken again.

Throughout the city, anyone awake and watching TV is learning that the criminal on the loose has finally been captured. Maybe they're learning that a boy from the other side of town helped catch him while he was babysitting for his rich uncle and aunt.

But no one is reporting the clown, Hamid guesses. He *imagined* the clown.

As Mo turns onto San Luis Avenue, Hamid sees someone on the pavement up ahead, walking in the rain.

He leans forward and squints through the sheets of rain on the windscreen.

As they drive down the avenue, Hamid sees that the man – with no umbrella and no coat – is wearing gloves.

White gloves.

They'll pass him soon. Hamid will have a good look at him then.

But the figure turns suddenly and grins madly at the oncoming SUV. At the last moment, he leaps into the street.

His mouth is red, and the skin around his eyes is painted white, including his eyelids. His hair is in two matted brick-red tufts, one at each ear.

"Mo, look out!" Hamid shouts. He leans across and grabs the steering wheel and jerks it hard to the right, sending the car up onto the pavement and into a recycling bin and a rubbish can.

Mo slams on the brakes and stops just before the car crashes into the front of a neighbourhood market.

Hamid watches out the driver window as the man runs to the far pavement and ducks around a corner.

"What are you doing?!" Mo snaps. He turns in his seat, and his face is red with anger. "You could have killed us!"

"It was him!" Hamid says. "You almost hit him!"

"Hit who?!" Mo says. "There was no one there, Hamid! The street is empty. It's the middle of the night and pouring! Who do you think is wandering the streets?"

"The clown!" Hamid shouts. He sounds crazy. He knows that. Maybe he *is* crazy. "It was the clown."

Mo takes a deep breath. The anger leaves his face and his voice. "Hamid," he says, his voice calmer now. "There was no one there. You probably dozed off for a minute. It's very late."

"I didn't–" Hamid starts to say, but he can't argue anymore. He's too tired. Maybe he did doze off. What else would he dream about? He'll probably be dreaming about that maniac clown for the rest of his life, just like the twins.

Mo throws the car into reverse. "Let's get you home now," he says. He pulls back onto the road and starts driving slowly along San Luis. "This has been a very long night. For everyone."

CHAPTER 12

Mo pulls up beside the kerb in front of Hamid's building. "Is your mum waiting up for you?" he asks.

Hamid shakes his head. He looks out the passenger window through the sheets of rain at the dull brownish-red block of flats where he lives with his mum. He half expects to see the clown huddled inside the entrance, waiting for him.

"She has to work in the morning," Hamid says.

"I'll wait to see you get inside all right," Mo says. "Oh wait, I almost forgot." He reaches into his pocket for money to pay Hamid.

"Don't worry about it," Hamid says. "You don't have to pay me."

"Come on," Mo says. "Don't be silly. It was a long night. And a rough night."

"Really, I don't want any money for this," Hamid says, popping his door open. "This wasn't exactly a normal babysitting night."

Before Mo can reply, Hamid is out of the car and closing the door behind him.

* * *

With the late night and the police and everything, plus the drive home, Hamid isn't in his own bed till after three in the morning. It's the latest he's ever been up, and he's exhausted.

He lies in his bed with the covers up to his chin and stares at the window. The shade is drawn, and the streetlights outside light up the pouring rain and cast eerie shadows of the raindrops that have landed on Hamid's bedroom window.

As he falls asleep, he wishes he could stop himself. He wishes he wouldn't fall asleep, because he hears the footsteps first. Then he hears a stifled snicker and a goofy laugh, and soon the laughter is loud and crazed.

His bedroom door creaks and opens. The laughter is louder, and that white-gloved hand reaches into the room. Then the clown is standing there at the foot of the bed, looking down at him, laughing and laughing.

Hamid doesn't know if he's asleep. Was he asleep at Julie and Mo's house? Is he having a nightmare because Ahmed and Afifa told him about theirs?

Was Ahmed right, and this is just a scary dream?

Was Afifa right, and the clown is here in his room right now?

Hamid can only stare up at him, at his painted red grin and his glaring white eyes. The make-up runs down his face now, wet from the pouring rain. His hair is limp and dripping at the sides of his head.

The clown snickers and giggles and steps closer and closer to Hamid's bed.

"You left me there," the clown hisses at him. His painted lips curve up into a wicked smile. "You left me there with Pryce, a dangerous maniac." His eyes narrow. "And I'd know," he whispers. "After all, it takes one to know one."

The clown stands up straight for a moment and laughs towards the ceiling. It's a loud and ridiculous laugh, like he's just said the funniest thing ever.

Hamid doesn't think it's funny. He moves back on the bed, so his back is all the way in the corner. He realizes he's sitting just like Pryce was when the police found him.

"Do you know what he would have done to me?" the clown whispers as he steps closer to Hamid's bed. "He wants to get back at me, you know, for what I did to him."

He's next to the bed now, so close that Hamid can see where the make-up has smeared on his face, revealing the pink colour of his cheeks.

"Do you want to know," he whispers, close enough now that Hamid can smell his breath, "what I did to him?"

All Hamid can do is sit up, close his eyes, and scream as loud as he can, hoping that this is a dream.

GLOSSARY

cackle laugh in a sharp, loud way

commentary description of or comments about an event

distraction something that makes it difficult to pay attention

high-definition technology that creates clear, detailed images

imagination ability to create new ideas and images in your mind, particularly of things that are not real

maniac person who acts in a violent, dangerous way

mischievous causing annoyance or harm in a playful way

obsession activity that a person spends a lot of time doing or thinking about

reassure make someone feel at ease

reluctantly done with hesitation

revered honoured or respected

stifled hold back or stop

translator one who helps change spoken or written words from one language into another

unbelievable impossible to believe or unlikely to be true

unstable showing quick changes in behaviour or mood

urgent requiring immediate action or attention

DISCUSSION QUESTIONS

1. In this story, did you believe Afifa, who said that the clown was real, or Ahmed, who claimed that the clown was part of a nightmare they both were having? Discuss who you believed – Afifa or Ahmed – and why.

2. Hamid isn't sure whether he actually saw the clown or whether he was dreaming. Have you ever had a dream that seemed like it was real life? Talk about why it was confusing.

3. Do you think that Aunt Julie and Uncle Mo did the right thing by telling Hamid that the police didn't believe him? What else could they have done? Discuss the possibilities.

WRITING PROMPTS

1. At the end of the story, Hamid is confronted by the clown once more. He wants to convince himself that he's dreaming, but he's not sure he is. Pretend you are Hamid, and write a paragraph or two describing your thoughts.

2. Imagine you are the newsreader for the local radio station. Write up an account of what happened at Aunt Julie and Uncle Mo's house and practise reporting it to a friend.

3. When Afifa tells Hamid about the clown, at first Hamid believes the twins are just having a nightmare, but later in the story, he changes his mind. Have you ever changed your mind about something? Write about it.

ABOUT THE AUTHOR

Eric Stevens lives in Minnesota, USA. He is studying to become a middle-school English teacher. Some of his favourite things include pizza, playing video games, watching cooking programmes on TV, riding his bike and trying new restaurants. Some of his least favourite things include olives and shovelling snow.

ABOUT THE ILLUSTRATOR

Nelson Evergreen lives on the south coast of the United Kingdom with his partner and their imaginary cat. Evergreen is a comic artist, illustrator and general all-round doodler of whatever nonsense pops into his head. He contributes regularly to the British underground comic scene, and he is currently writing and illustrating a number of graphic novel and picture book hybrids for older children.

NIGHT-TIME HORRORS

Escaped prisoners and creepy clowns are certainly scary, but what's even more terrifying are the things that may be lurking in our very own dreams. What causes frightening visions to interrupt our peaceful slumber? Myths and science alike attempt to explain the night-time horrors.

According to German folklore, an evil spirit called a mare (probably from an ancient word meaning "to harm", *mare* forms part of the word nightmare) creeps into your room and sits on your chest. The mare torments you throughout the night by giving you nightmares.

Many cultures around the world tell similar stories of evil nocturnal creatures that cause unrestful sleep. Sometimes they sit on the sleeper's chest. Other times they strangle the sleeper, and in rare cases, they even slowly suck the life out of the unsuspecting person.

Folktales of these nightmare-causing beings are probably a way that people explained a phenomenon known today as sleep paralysis. Have you ever woken up in the middle of the night so scared you couldn't move? You might have experienced sleep paralysis. Sleep paralysis happens just as you fall asleep or wake up and causes you to be unable to move temporarily.

People who experience sleep paralysis often report terrifying visions – commonly an overwhelming feeling that an intruder has entered the room. Although it doesn't cause any health problems, sleep paralysis is very unpleasant and can be extremely terrifying.

Part of what can be so frightening about a nightmare is how real it feels. You may even think you woke up, only to still be in the world of the dream. This is known as a false awakening, or a dream within a dream. You could also have drifted asleep and into a dream while still believing you're awake. Mind tricks such as this make the task of distinguishing dreams from reality even more difficult.

Was Hamid letting his imagination get the best of him? Was he just dreaming? Whether what visits us at night is real or only a bad dream, the terror that remains is very, very real.

SPINE SHIVERS

THE SCREAMING BRIDGE

BY J. A. DARKE

THE SCREAMING BRIDGE

Emma ran, finding her way by the moonlight, until her lungs burned. When she finally stopped, she doubled over, hands on her knees, gasping for air.

Long minutes passed. Emma stood shaking, not sure if she could continue. She had no idea where she was anymore. She couldn't see any roads or trails or the river. She was lost in the darkness.

Where is the road? she wondered. *Oh no. I ... I should have stayed on the road, and now I'm lost ... and where are my friends?*

The tears came easily then in loud, choking sobs that made her fall to her knees on the ground.

Emma sat down and pulled her legs up to her chest. Her feet were cold, but strangely, her trainers were no longer wet. Her jeans were torn and smeared with dirt and blood from her scraped palms.

I can't stay here all night, she thought as she shivered from the cold breeze. *I have to keep moving.*

She got to her feet and turned in circles, searching for any sign of civilization. A farm. A car. A road. She pulled her phone out of her pocket, doubting that it would somehow be charged and working.

She was right. It was still dead.

Past a large thicket of trees on her left, Emma spied a section of the night sky that seemed a bit hazier than the rest, as if from the collective glow of a thousand lights.

That must be Sterling, Emma thought as she began to walk in that direction.

When Emma entered the canopy of trees,

she ducked to avoid a low-hanging branch. She walked with her arms in front of her for safety. Dead leaves and twigs crunched and cracked beneath her trainers like dried, brittle bones.

As she reached the other side of the thicket, Emma saw a flicker of light dance in the corner of her eye. She pushed aside an evergreen branch and strained to see the light's source.

Far in the distance, a set of headlights cut through the black night.

A road, she thought. *That must be a road.*

Emma felt a renewed strength wash over her. She burst out of the trees, into a ditch filled with large boulders and weeds. She climbed over the rocks quickly but cautiously, so as not to twist an ankle.

When she reached the top of the ditch, Emma stumbled out onto the road, right into the glare of oncoming headlights. She instinctively scrambled back to the shoulder of the road as the car's driver slammed on the brakes, and the vehicle swerved on the loose gravel.

The car stopped about a metre away from Emma.

Out of breath, she slowly lowered herself to the ground, exhausted. She looked up and tried to see the driver of the car, but all she could make out was the driver's silhouette as he exited the vehicle.

The car door slammed. "Emma! Oh, thank goodness, it's you!"

"Connor?" Emma whispered. She didn't believe it. It couldn't be him.

Could it?

A second door opened, followed by Lucy's voice. "Em! Are you all right?"

Lucy ran to Emma, fell to her knees in the gravel beside her, and hugged her close.

It really is Lucy, Emma thought. *She's warm, so warm ... and dry.*

And most importantly, she was *alive*.

Emma hugged her friend fiercely. Her head was a cloud of confusion. She had so many questions. But for the moment, all she wanted to do was remain on the ground with Lucy.

Daniel exited the car as well and walked over to the group. When Emma was finally ready to stand, he held his hand out, offering to help her to her feet.

"Thanks," Emma said to Daniel as he pulled her up from the ground.

"Let's go to the car," he said. "You're shaking like a leaf."

He put his arm around Emma's shoulders and walked with her to the car. She hesitated before climbing into the backseat, expecting to see the ghost of the little girl with the necklace waiting for her.

But the car was dry, like nothing had happened.

How is that possible? she wondered.

"Are you okay?" Daniel asked.

"I'm ... I'm fine," Emma lied. Then she eased herself into the backseat.

Daniel started to get into the car next to her, but Lucy cut him off. "I'll sit with her," she said, climbing in beside Emma and taking her hand.

"Roll the windows down," Emma whispered. Claustrophobia was creeping in on her, making it hard to breathe.

"What?" Lucy asked.

"The windows," Emma repeated. "Open them. Leave them open. Please?"

From the driver's seat, Connor said, "Yeah. Of course, Em."

For a time, the journey back to Sterling was silent. The wind from the open windows was brisk and cold and made the two girls shiver even as they huddled together in the backseat.

Finally, Lucy asked, "Emma, what happened?"

She didn't know where to begin. She stumbled over her words. "I – I saw them … the ghosts. First I heard the screams … then we were trapped in the car … and then …" She trailed off.

"Trapped in the car?" Lucy asked, confused. "Emma, what do you mean? We were never trapped in the car."

SPINE SHIVERS